NEW ENGLAND PATRIOTS

ALL-TIME GREATS

BY TED COLEMAN

Book design by Jake Slavik
Cover design by Jake Slavik

Photographs ©: Chris Cecere/AP Images, cover (top), 1 (top); Damian Strohmeyer/AP Images, cover (bottom), 1 (bottom); Tony Tomsic/AP Images, 4, 8; Ian Johnson/Icon Sportswire, 7; Mike Kullen/AP Images, 11; Hector Acevedo/Zuma Press/Icon Sportswire, 13; Richard C. Lewis/Icon Sportswire, 14; Gregory Fisher/Icon Sportswire, 15; Pro Football Hall of Fame/AP Images, 16; Tomasso DeRosa/AP Images, 18; Paul Kuroda/Zuma Press/Icon Sportswire, 21

Press Box Books, an imprint of Press Room Editions.

ISBN
978-1-63494-360-4 (library bound)
978-1-63494-377-2 (paperback)
978-1-63494-410-6 (epub)
978-1-63494-394-9 (hosted ebook)

Library of Congress Control Number: 2020952638

Distributed by North Star Editions, Inc.
2297 Waters Drive
Mendota Heights, MN 55120
www.northstareditions.com

Printed in the United States of America
082021

ABOUT THE AUTHOR

Ted Coleman is a sportswriter who lives in Louisville, Kentucky, with his trusty Affenpinscher, Chloe.

TABLE OF CONTENTS

PARILLI
15

CHAPTER 1

SUPER QUARTERBACKS

For their first 25 seasons, the Patriots were known mostly for losing. Even so, the Patriots had some great quarterbacks during that time. **Babe Parilli** joined the team in 1961. Back then, they were known as the Boston Patriots, and they played in the American Football League (AFL). Parilli had his best season in 1964, when he threw 31 touchdown passes. That set a team record that stood for more than four decades.

Steve Grogan came along in 1975. By that point, the AFL had merged with the National Football League (NFL). Grogan lost his starting job to Tony Eason in the 1980s. But when Eason struggled in 1985, Grogan came back to win six games in a row. Eason and Grogan split quarterback duties in 1985. And the Patriots reached their first Super Bowl that season. However, it ended in a blowout loss to the Chicago Bears.

The Patriots didn't return to the Super Bowl until the 1996 season. **Drew Bledsoe** was the quarterback by then. He broke many of Grogan's team records. When he

BILL BELICHICK

Head coach **Bill Belichick** played just as big a role in the Patriots' success as the players did. Belichick became New England's head coach in 2000. He went 5–11 that year. But Belichick didn't have another losing record for the next 19 years. He won six Super Bowls during that stretch. Belichick established himself as one of the greatest coaches in NFL history.

got hurt in the 2001 season, it seemed like the Patriots were doomed.

But in came **Tom Brady**. Few players in NFL history have had such a big impact on their team. During his 20 seasons with the Patriots, Brady led New England to nine Super Bowls. He won six of them. Brady also won three Most Valuable Player (MVP) awards and tossed 541 touchdown passes as a Patriot. Many football fans consider him the greatest player of all time.

NANCE
35

CHAPTER 2
BACKS AND RECEIVERS

During their early years, the Patriots had several memorable players on offense. **Gino Cappelletti** came to the Patriots as a kicker and defensive back in 1960. But he turned into a great receiver. He was named the league MVP in 1964.

Running the ball was star fullback **Jim Nance**. Weighing in at 260 pounds, Nance was known for his size and strength. But he also had enough speed to rack up the yardage. In 1966, Nance earned the league's MVP award.

Nance scored more rushing touchdowns than any other player in team history. However, **Sam Cunningham** ran for more yards. Cunningham was a key part of the 1978 Patriots. That team set an NFL record for most rushing yards.

New England's all-time leading receiver played during this era, too. **Stanley Morgan** is still the only Patriot with 10,000 receiving yards. And he did it on a team that was best known for running the ball. Morgan played through the 1980s and appeared in the Super Bowl after the 1985 season.

STAT SPOTLIGHT

CAREER RUSHING YARDS

PATRIOTS TEAM RECORD

Sam Cunningham: 5,453

MORGAN
86

Receiver **Troy Brown** had his only 1,000-yard season in 2001. But he was an outstanding returner. Brown had a memorable punt return for a touchdown in the conference title game during the 2001 season. Brown was a member of three championship teams. He is New England's all-time leader in punt returns.

Tight end **Ben Coates** set the standard for Patriots tight ends. He racked up 50 touchdowns from 1991 to 1999. But his records were crushed by **Rob Gronkowski**. "Gronk" was tall, fast, and strong. He could

SUPER LINEMEN

Each Patriots Super Bowl team had a standout on the offensive line. **John Hannah** played his final season in 1985. He reached the Super Bowl that season and made his ninth Pro Bowl. **Bruce Armstrong** played from 1987 to 2000. He made six Pro Bowls. And **Logan Mankins** played from 2005 to 2013. He made six Pro Bowls as a Patriot.

GRONKOWSKI
87

outrun his opponents, but he could also run them over. Gronkowski scored 80 touchdowns from 2010 to 2018.

Tom Brady loved quick receivers with great hands. He had two of the best in

Wes Welker and **Julian Edelman**. Welker had been a backup with the Miami Dolphins. But the Patriots made him a starter in 2007. Welker notched 1,000-yard seasons in all but one of his six seasons in New England.

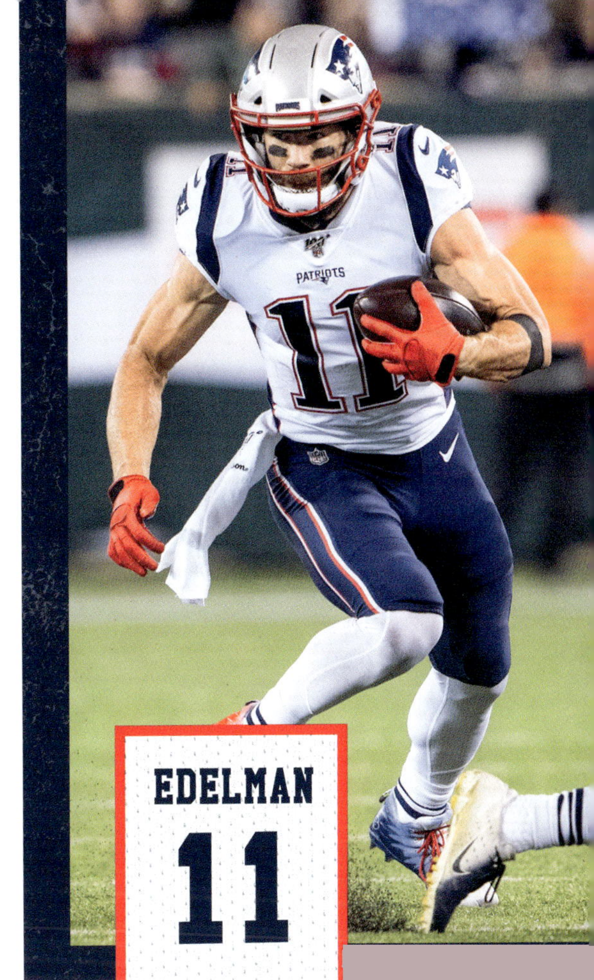

Edelman became Brady's top target after Welker left. Edelman's career highlight came during the Super Bowl in the 2018 season. He had 141 receiving yards in that game. Edelman earned Super Bowl MVP honors, and the Patriots won their sixth title.

HAYNES
40

CHAPTER 3

PATRIOT DEFENDERS

In the 1960s, defensive tackle **Jim Lee Hunt** was known as "Earthquake." When Hunt battled his way through the offensive line, the ground seemed to shake. Hunt was also known for his quickness. He recovered many fumbles during his career.

In the late 1970s and early 1980s, few cornerbacks were better than **Mike Haynes**. He recorded 28 interceptions as a Patriot. He was also an excellent punt returner. Haynes spent seven seasons with New England. And he made the Pro Bowl in six of them.

In the 1980s, linebacker **Andre Tippett** was nearly unstoppable. Tippett could tackle runners, but he was best known as a sack machine. He had 100 sacks during his 11-year career. That was a team record.

The 1996 Patriots Super Bowl team had two defensive players who would become longtime Patriots. Linebacker **Tedy Bruschi** was a rookie that year. He went on to win three Super Bowl rings with New England.

Bruschi suffered a stroke in 2005 but came back and played four more years.

Cornerback **Ty Law** was in his second year in 1996. He quickly became the defender that opposing quarterbacks avoided. Law won three Super Bowls on the same teams as Bruschi. He also tied for the most interceptions in Patriots history.

Willie McGinest lined up at both linebacker and defensive end. He was at his best in the playoffs. McGinest recorded 16 career playoff sacks. That was the most in NFL history. McGinest also won three rings with Law and Bruschi.

STAT SPOTLIGHT

CAREER INTERCEPTIONS

PATRIOTS TEAM RECORD

Ty Law and Raymond Clayborn (tie): 36

Defensive tackle **Vince Wilfork** joined the team in 2004. The Patriots were already champions at that point. And Wilfork helped the defense stay at a Super Bowl level. Strong and powerful, Wilfork stuffed runners and sacked quarterbacks.

Cornerback **Stephon Gilmore** led the next generation of great Patriots defenders. Gilmore joined the team in 2017, his sixth NFL season. But he reached new heights in New England. Gilmore tied for the league lead in interceptions in 2019. He was also named Defensive Player of

THE SPECIALISTS

From 1996 to 2019, the Patriots had just two kickers. **Adam Vinatieri** and **Stephen Gostkowski** were two of the most accurate kickers of all time. Vinatieri was especially good in clutch situations. He made the game-winning kick in two Super Bowls.

the Year. After Tom Brady left in 2020, Patriots fans hoped the team's defense would help New England stay on top.

TIMELINE

1960
1970
1980
1990
2000
2010
2020
JIM LEE HUNT
(1960–70)
GINO CAPPELLETTI
(1960–70)
JIM NANCE
(1965–71)
BABE PARILLI
(1961–1967)
SAM CUNNINGHAM
(1973–79, 1981–82)
STEVE GROGAN
(1975–90)
MIKE HAYNES
(1976–82)
STANLEY MORGAN
(1977–89)
ANDRE TIPPETT
(1982–88, 1990–93)
BEN COATES
(1991–99)
DREW BLEDSOE
(1993–2001)
TROY BROWN
(1993–2007)
WILLIE McGINEST
(1994–2005)
TY LAW
(1995–2004)
TEDY BRUSCHI
(1996–2008)
TOM BRADY
(2000–19)
VINCE WILFORK
(2004–14)
WES WELKER
(2007–12)
JULIAN EDELMAN
(2009–20)
ROB GRONKOWSKI
(2010–18)
STEPHON GILMORE
(2017–)

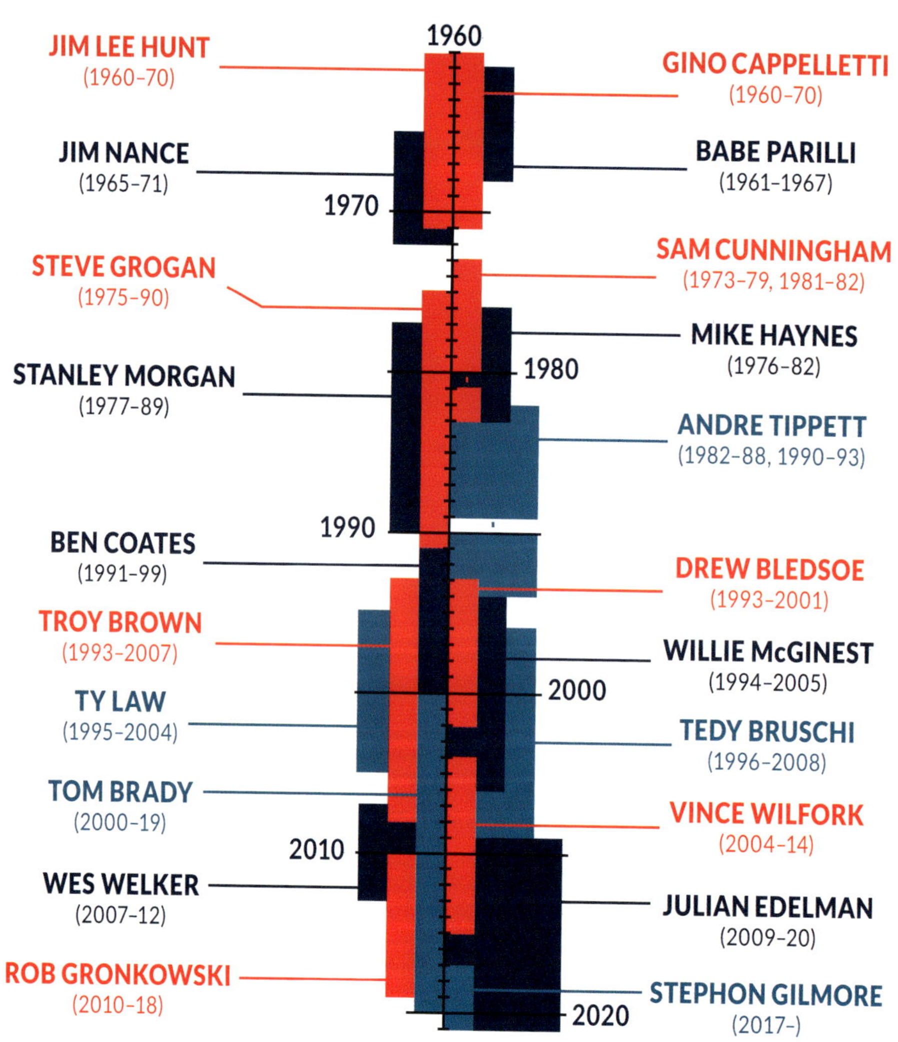

TEAM FACTS

NEW ENGLAND PATRIOTS

Founded: 1960

Formerly: Boston Patriots (1960–70)

Super Bowl titles: 6 (2001, 2003, 2004, 2014, 2016, 2018)*

Key coaches:

Mike Holovak (1961–68), 52–46–9

Raymond Berry (1984–89), 48–39–0

Bill Belichick (2000–), 244–92–0, 6 Super Bowl titles

MORE INFORMATION

To learn more about the New England Patriots, go to **pressboxbooks.com/AllAccess**

These links are routinely monitored and updated to provide the most current information available.

**1966 through 2020*

GLOSSARY

clutch
Having to do with a difficult situation when the outcome of the game is in question.

conference
A subset of teams within a sports league.

cornerback
A defensive player who covers wide receivers near the sidelines.

linebacker
A player who lines up behind the defensive linemen and in front of the defensive backs.

Pro Bowl
The NFL's all-star game, in which the league's best players compete.

sack
A tackle of the quarterback behind the line of scrimmage.

tight end
An offensive player who blocks but can also catch passes.

INDEX